Bonito the Hero

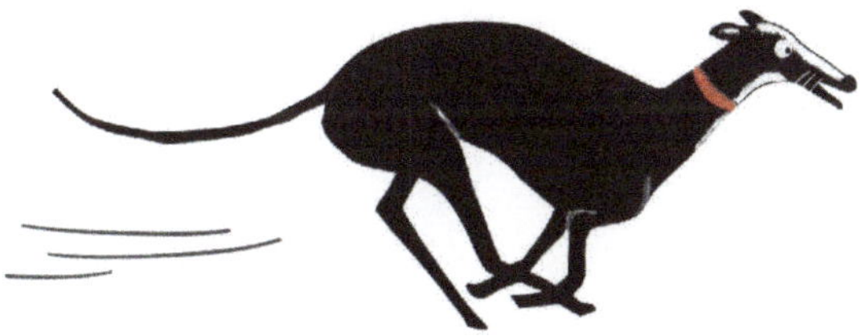

FIELD

For Roxanne

Published by Poppy Seed Publishers Limited
32A Moreton End Lane
Harpenden
AL5 2HD
poppyseedpub@gmail.com

ISBN: 978-1-9993499-6-7

Poppy Seed
PUBLISHERS

Bonito the Hero

by Natalie Knox

Poppy Seed
PUBLISHERS

Bonito is a handsome Spanish greyhound who loves lying in the sun. His black shiny coat glistens, his white racing stripe shines, and his long whippy tail stretches out behind him. His favourite dreams these days are about running. But sometimes he dreams about guns, a hungry tummy and those scary green jackets. When he wakes up, he sighs happily because he remembers he is safe in his new home.

Pedro takes Bonito for a walk every morning. It's always the same ...

Head down the hill to the bins. Turn right at the red brick wall where the sniffy boxer lives. Carry on to the lamppost, read all the neighbourhood news, and greet the bouncy fox terrier. Cross the road at the big tree where the hairy German shepherd appears through the bottom of the hedge, and on past the flowerbeds.

At the house with the cute collie pup, turn left and tug all the way to the open field.

When Pedro unleashes him, Bonito bounds forward and pants,

I'm trim,
I'm slim,
I'm built for speed.
I'll dash and flash,
when off the lead.

Today, Bonito takes his time at the lamppost. There were puppies born two streets over! The fox terrier has a vet appointment today, and the collie pup wonders why the suitcases are down from the attic. Bonito adds a note saying the field has been mowed.

When Bonito uncurls from his nap, it's afternoon and the children are home. The garden is full of noise and happiness. He can't resist the bumble tumble of their joyful games and zooms round and round the garden. This makes them squeal with delight and clap their hands.

He yaps,

I'm trim,
I'm slim,
I'm built for speed.
I'll dash and flash,
when off the lead.

ARF!

The next day, there are fresh messages on the lamppost. Something called fireworks are happening tonight and everyone is frightened. The German shepherd said he's hiding under the bed. The boxer said he hopes he gets the sleepy medicine again and the fox terrier said he'll probably go hoarse with barking. Bonito doesn't feel too good about fireworks. He wonders if it's anything like those scary green jackets.

After dark, there are loud banging sounds in the sky. BANG! BANG! BANG!

He's not afraid of the noise. It reminds him of his old life with the hunters. There were always loud bangs from the guns. He remembers the thrill of chasing rabbits, but then he also remembers being hungry and having sore feet. He remembers being afraid of those green jackets.

Hang on ... what can he hear?

The fox terrier has raised the alarm. It's the collie pup! She's bolted in fright. He can sense how terrified the other dogs are. He may be afraid of jackets, but he's not afraid of fireworks! He'll go and find the pup because ...

I'm trim,
I'm slim,
I'm built for speed.
I'll dash and flash,
when off the lead.

Past the red brick wall, the lamppost and flowerbeds. On to the field and wide, open space. Bonito's eyes are focused, his nose is alert. He picks up the scent of the pup and sprints with all his might. YES! He can see her in the distance.

“STOP!”

Bonito skids next to the panting pup.
“I’m here, you’re not alone, little one.”
The collie is shivering, and Bonito moves closer.
He waits as the pup calms.

“I was so afraid, I felt like I had to escape,”
whispers the pup.
“I know what that feels like,” responds Bonito.
“Let’s get you home, where it’s safe.”

The next morning, Pedro and Bonito head out early. Down the hill to the bins and left at the red brick wall. At the lamppost, Bonito is surprised to read so many messages. Some say thank you for rescuing the collie pup. Others say he is a hero. Across the road to the big tree and on past the flowerbeds.

Is he a hero?

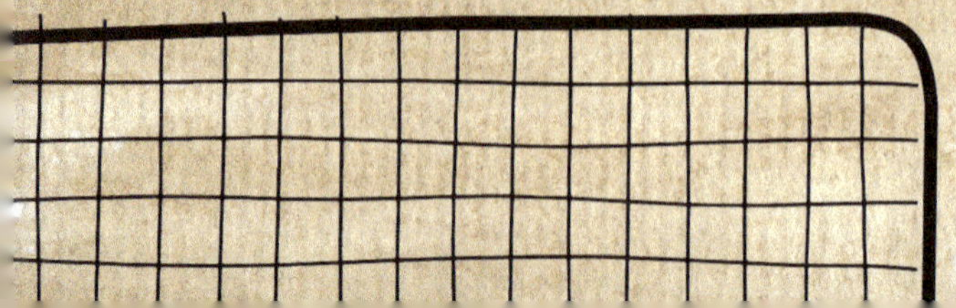

A hero's rescue!
Thank you!
hero!!
You saved her!
HERO!

Tug all the way to the open field, and, finally free ...

I'm trim, I'm slim,
I'm glad I ran.
I'll dash and flash,
I'm glad I can.

I'm slim, I'm trim,
I'm glad I saved.
I dashed, I flashed,
the fire I braved.

FIELD

Milton Keynes UK
Ingram Content Group UK Ltd.
UKHW051710030324
438679UK00005B/10

9 781999 349967